This Little Tiger book
belongs to:

_____

_____

_____

For Ben and Tom, with love
~ J. R.

For Ethan, who surprised
everyone by being so early
~ T. W.

LITTLE TIGER PRESS
An imprint of Magi Publications
1 The Coda Centre, 189 Munster Road, London SW6 6AW
www.littletigerpress.com

First published in Great Britain 2005
This edition published 2006

A CIP catalogue record for this book is available from the British Library

Printed in Malaysia by Tien Wah Press Pte.

2 4 6 8 10 9 7 5 3 1

Rosie's Special Surprise

Julia Rawlinson   *illustrated by* Tim Warnes

LITTLE TIGER PRESS
London

Nosy Rosie liked to know everything about everything, but Daddy Rabbit was planning a special surprise. Nosy Rosie kept trying to guess what it could be, but Daddy Rabbit only smiled and said, "Wait and see."

But Nosy Rosie didn't wait.
While the other rabbits
slept, she hopped out of
the burrow.

Through the meadow,
across the stream
and up the hill
hopped Nosy Rosie.

Brushing buttercups,
over the clover, under
the sun she hopped.
Round a big tree,
round a small tree,
over a log she hopped.

And behind the
log she found . . .

. . . a store of acorns,
hidden in a hollow.

"That's not your surprise," chattered
a scampery-skippity squirrel.
 "Do you know what my surprise is?" asked
Nosy Rosie, bouncing up and down.
 "Yes. It is shaped a little bit like an acorn,"
said the squirrel. Then he scampered off with
some twigs, and Nosy Rosie bounced on again.

She asked the butterflies and
the bees if they'd seen her surprise.
She asked the sheep and the cows
if they had seen it.

She asked the mice and
the moles if they had seen
it. And as she asked the
moles she saw . . .

. . . a secret entrance to their tunnel. "That's not your surprise," snuffled the burrowy-tunnelly moles.

"Do you know what my surprise is?" asked Nosy Rosie, hopping around. "Yes. It's not a tunnel, but you can go in it," said the moles. Then they burrowed off to dig up roots from the ground.

Under stones and snail shells and bits of twig searched Nosy Rosie. Through the dippled, dappled sunshine of the wood she searched.

In amongst the straggly
tangles of the hedge she
searched. And in the
hedge she found . . .

. . . a nest full of speckled eggs.
  "That's not your surprise," chirruped
the flittering-fluttering birds.

"Do you know what my surprise is?" asked Nosy Rosie, sniffing the breeze.

"Yes. It is blue, a little bit like our eggs," said Daddy Bird. Then he gathered up some moss and fluttered off through the trees.

Nosy Rosie bounced on,
up a steep hill. She found
a stone shaped like an
acorn, but that wasn't her
surprise. She found a ferny
hollow she could go in,
but that wasn't it.

She found a flower
as blue as a bird's egg,
but that wasn't it.
Where could her surprise
be? Nosy Rosie stood high
on tiptoes. She looked out
over the woods and . . .

. . . tumbled down,
down, down.
Down the hill,
roly-poly,
head-over-toes
went Nosy Rosie.
Bumpity, bumpity,
up in the air and
down on her tail
went Nosy Rosie.
Slipping and sliding,
skidding and
skittering,
four paws flying
went Nosy Rosie.

Into a heap with a bump and
a thud and a last little thump
went Nosy Rosie.

Then she sat up, twitched her ears
and gave a sad little snuffle.
"I'm never going to find this thing,"
she said, brushing earth from her fur.
"I'm tired of looking and hopping," she
said, rubbing her bumped bunny nose.

"Too tired for your surprise?"
asked Daddy Rabbit, bouncing up.
"Come with me and see . . .

". . . your huge blue balloon of a surprise!
Jump in and ride with me."
"Ooh, thank you, thank you!" said
Nosy Rosie, bouncing in.

"Now I can see
the whole wide
world, I can see . . ."

"... EVERYTHING!"

More special surprises from Little Tiger Press

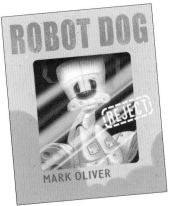

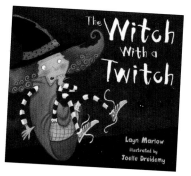

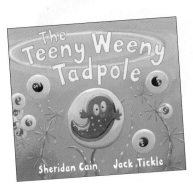

For information regarding any of the above
titles or for our catalogue, please contact us:
Little Tiger Press, 1 The Coda Centre,
189 Munster Road, London SW6 6AW
Tel: 020 7385 6333 Fax: 020 7385 7333
E-mail: info@littletiger.co.uk www.littletigerpress.com